THE PSYCHOPATH'S NOTEBOOK

To Know - To Will
To Dare - To Be Silent

IN FOUR PARTS

by
Christopher S. Hyatt, Ph.D.

Illustrated by S. Jason Black

THE *Original* FALCON PRESS
TEMPE, ARIZONA, U.S.A.

Copyright © 2004 CE by Christopher S. Hyatt, Ph.D.

All rights reserved. No part of this book, in part or in whole, may be reproduced, transmitted, or utilized, in any form or by any means, electronic or mechanical, including photocopying, recording, or by any information storage and retrieval system, without permission in writing from the publisher, except for brief quotations in critical articles, books and reviews.

International Standard Book Number: 978-1-935150-44-2

First Edition 2004
Second Printing 2007
Third Printing 2008

Address all inquiries to:
THE ORIGINAL FALCON PRESS
1753 East Broadway Road #101-277
Tempe, AZ 85282 U.S.A.
(or)
PO Box 3540
Silver Springs NV 89429 U.S.A.
website: http://www.originalfalcon.com
email: info@originalfalcon.com

TABLE OF CONTENTS

Foreword 5
Introduction 6
A Bit of Background... 7
Part 1: The Extreme Types 11
Part 2: The Joys of Revenge 26
Part 3: A Day in the Life of A Psychopath............................. 28
Part 4: The Seven Blessings, Often Called The Seven Deadly
    Sins 34

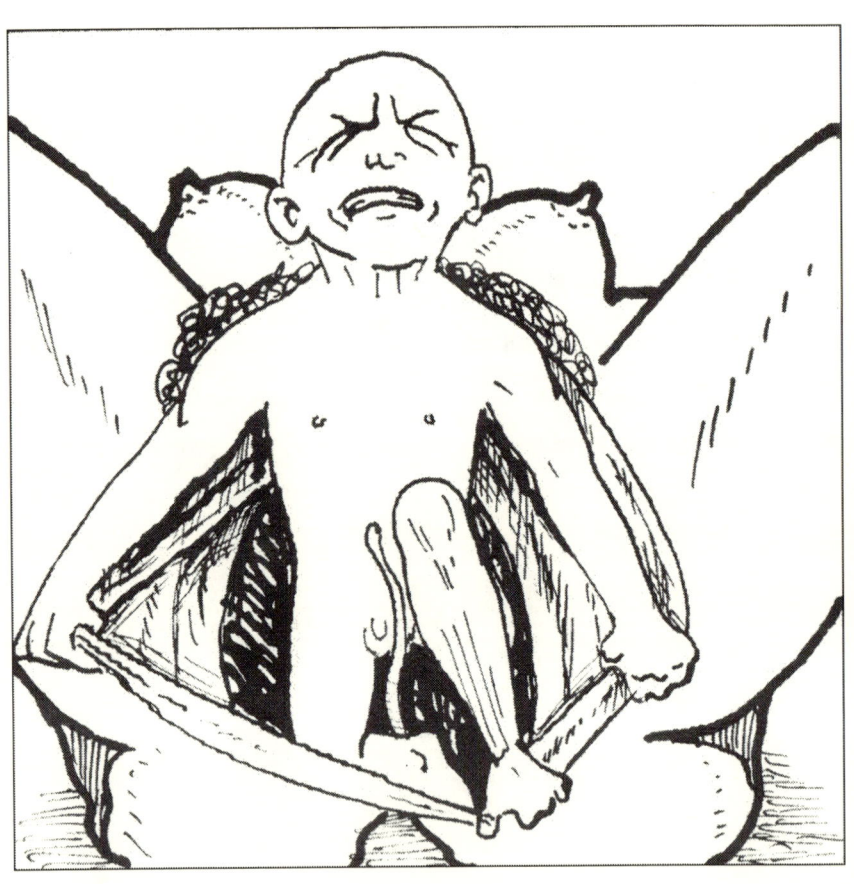

FOREWORD

What is this all about?

It's about four types of Individuals.

By understanding these types you will be able to quickly analyze the various people you meet, and apply different methods of operation.

The method of teaching is as usual: I provide some basic information and you do the work. The information is supplied in a number of forms—thus communicating to the various parts and pieces of the brain.

And, as usual, you must first apply the knowledge to yourself and those close to you.

Repetition and experience are the basic keys to becoming a competent operative.

Note: Be prepared for your exam on this material.

INTRODUCTION

From many years of research, anecdotal evidence, observation and literature review, I have postulated four basic types of people.

I will not argue here whether what I have suggested is caused by genetics, child rearing, culture, luck, or trauma; all that I am concerned with here are the basic types, what I call The Magician, The Emperor, The Hermit and The Universe.

Keep in mind that simply because a person is a particular type doesn't mean that under unusual or stressful situations they will not demonstrate some of the behavior of another type.

There is nothing new about types—Jung had his, Sheldon had his, and, of course, there is the work of Eysenck, Maslow and others—and there are numerous popular books describing temperaments. However, my interest is not in simple pathology—astro-types, genetic types or archetypes *per se*—but, rather, in the *Extreme* type: the future man which I often call The Psychopath—or sometimes have referred to as The Newman, or Superman......

A BIT OF BACKGROUND

Rats, Rats, Rats, and More Rats
A Rodent's Life—Renfield's Account

In my laboratory research utilizing lower animals, using sensory deprivation and pain, I found a number of interesting patterns. (These rats were from the same strain, keeping genetic differences to a minimum.)

The variables I manipulated were: deprivation of stimuli, the employment of electroshock, and food.

It was interesting to see that some animals became so hungry for stimuli that they would shock themselves even if food were not contingent on their pressing the famed "Skinner-Bar."

Under certain conditions the animals were aroused and explored their environment—they seemed to be having fun.

Under different circumstances these same animals were aroused but nervous—they were on guard, bored, not having fun……

I noticed two other conditions as well. Some animals were tired but tense—they had a hard time relaxing and were agitated. And, finally, there were some animals that were peacefully relaxed.

In another major study on conflict, my colleagues and I found that the spatial factors (cubic area) where the conflict was conditioned, permanently affected how the conditioned "neurosis" expressed itself. Primarily, the animals were either quiet and tense, or they were tense and hyperactive. Being anthropomorphic, we privately called what we created "depressive rats" and "manic rats." (We didn't use these terms in the published articles, but instead used symbols to represent the process of learning to be "crazy.")

I also noticed that some animals were prone to these various states at different times of the day, indicating an interaction between cycles and conflict.

These studies were published in peer-reviewed journals; therefore I was not free to speculate on my private observations or on other tentative observations as these were serendipitous observations adjunctive to the more specific purposes of these studies……

In private I speculated that these animals exhibited four extreme states of activity and, though there were four basic types, the various types actually existed on two continua (energy level and tension)......much like an equal-armed cross.

The published studies were significant enough to warrant a full fellowship to study at either of two major foreign (none USA) universities under the directorship of world-recognized experts on arousal, conflict and cognition.

The Human Side of Things

Just in case you think that I am inappropriately generalizing from rats to humans, I will tell you two stories.

When I was doing an internship at a State Hospital in California for the Mentally Impaired, I found that certain types of brain-damaged patients could tolerate and even enjoy an array of complex stimuli while others would find the same stimuli stressful. While not scientific, or in any way conclusive, it did remind me of my earlier rat research.

Jumping ahead a few years, as a psychotherapist I found some interesting types of patients:

What I have come to call the High-Tension, Low-Energy Type (or The Hermit) was sort of placid, often thin but could be overweight; they frequently exhibited the famous limp handshake; some even had sweaty palms. (In passing, the other day I met a very intelligent physician who, when I shook his hand, felt as if his hand were not connected to the rest of his body.)

These individuals reported that they were often tense and tired when trying to sleep. In doing some testing using a number of ego-strength scales, I found that these people had lower ego-strength than the High-Energy, High-Tension patients—The Emperor.

Using a number of self-rating scales on self-esteem, I found The Hermit to have lower reported self-esteem than the Emperor...... In addition, the Hermit tended to report more eccentric or bizarre life experiences. And while both groups lied......the Emperor showed more extremes in their lying score—they either almost always lied or almost never lied.

The High-Tension, High-Energy people (The Emperor) were more overtly aggressive—and in some cases could be made to fly off the handle rather easily...... They also liked their alcohol......

On the other hand, The Hermit was verbally hostile, sarcastic, passive-aggressive, and a saboteur.

The third type I called the normal average person (The Universe): rather low energy and moderate tension. They were the average man on the street who, in some cases, were very intelligent and held high-paying positions—but in essence were average both in their interests and their problems.

Finally, the fourth type (The Magician) has high energy and low tension. As a psychotherapist I rarely saw this type......in fact I can only remember one, and that was because he was extracting himself from a rather hysterical but highly attractive wife, and needed my assistance to get her off his back. I have met types like these in other contexts, some operating as high-level business owners; others were adventurers; and still others as leaders.

I would call these individuals both rare and healthy specimens—reflecting possibly some of the types to emerge through evolution and/or genetic manipulation.

I am defining health and illness in this context as:

Health relates to specific reactions to contextual situations with minimal effect to the deeper identity and general esteem structures which are strong and vigorous...

Illness refers to lower order reactions to contextual situations with moderate to maximal effect to the deeper identity and esteem structures which tend to be weak or fragile...

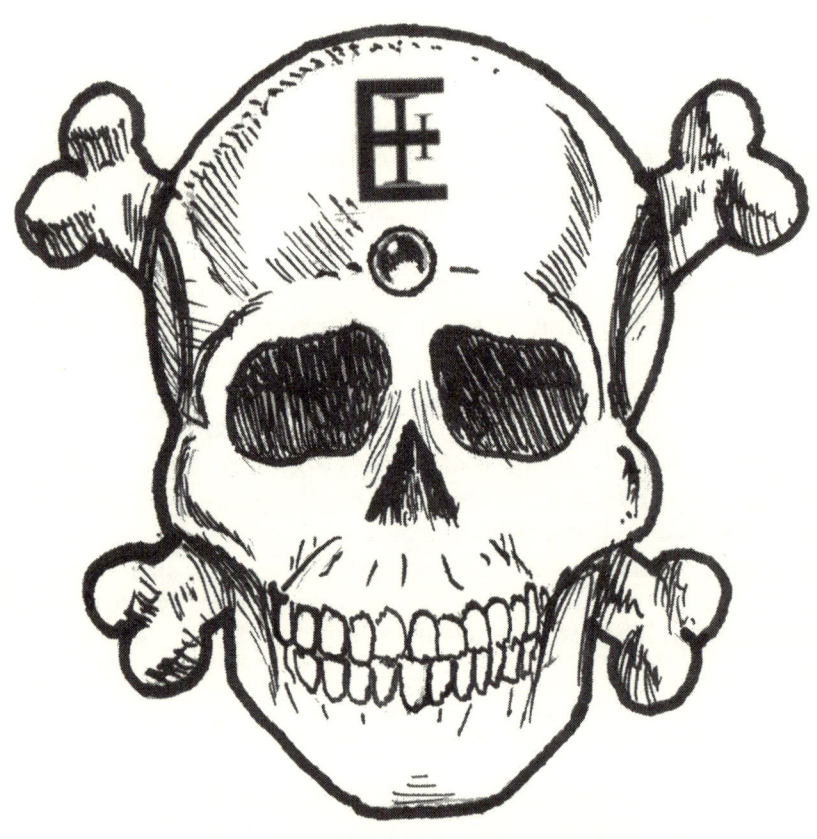

**To Know - To Will
To Dare - To Be Silent**

Part 1

THE EXTREME TYPES

1) **The Magician**
2) **The Emperor**
3) **The Hermit**
4) **The Universe**

Type A Person:
THE MAGICIAN

Genesis

This is our goal, the end result of Undoing or the simple luck of the draw. For me, this is the True Extreme Individual: the True Psychopath.

High Energy— Low Tension—

Cognition:
Good cognitive tone—
Tension, charge, discharge and relaxation—
Excellent access to rudimentary cognition———
Cognitive flexibility
Minimal beliefs
Contextual problem solving and expression—
Not lost in idealistic abstractions—
Cognition leads to action and accomplishment
Rational thinking
Creative thinking—
Access to various brain functions
Conscious perception with full awareness. The almost instant ability for understanding by which newly observed qualities of an object and related concepts are related and integrated with past experience.
Excellent imagination—goal directed
Non-compensatory fantasy life
Excellent ability to assess a situation and assess resources available
Instructs by example
Solid body image

Will:
Vigorous
Directed
Determined
Persistent

Strong but flexible
Warm self-discipline

Sensory—Tonic:
Non-chronic tension—
Capable of deep relaxation—
Good muscle tone—
Less affected by extraneous Bio-rhythms
Requires minimal sleep
Physically talented
Good Health

Emotion:
High frustration tolerance—
Very comfortable in one's own skin
Not drug or substance dependent—
Tolerates obstacles and responds productively
Minimal depression or aggression
If an error occurs, apologizes and fixes the situation as required
Active—expressive—open to life—
Does not explain oneself away
Low autonomic reactivity
The ability to experience a sense of wonderment and oneness without transforming the experience into metaphysics
Pleasant, easy-going, but firm

Evaluate yourself as this type.
Where are you on this 7 point scale?
Excellent — — — — — — Poor

Return to the top of this list and check mark the descriptions under each of the categories which apply to you. Now count the number of check marks and enter the number here: _____

Type B Person:
THE EMPEROR

High Energy—
High Tension—

Cognition:
Sloppy cognitive tone
Tension, charge, inadequate discharge, poor relaxation
Cognitive inflexibility—
Hyper-vigilant
Tendency toward obsession
Can be a true believer
Tendency toward irrationality, rigid thinking—
Hyper-critical—
Compensatory fantasy life
Can get lost in endless abstractions
Over-intellectualized
Messianic fantasy
Idealist
Exaggerated ability to assess a situation and resources available
Good apperception
Idealizes people and then often degrades them if disappointed
Tendency toward paranoia
Teaches by threats—i.e., authority
Hard and fractured body image

Will:
Stubborn
Bull in the china closet
Rigid-Crushable
Forced harsh discipline

Sensory—Tonic:
Poor ability to relax—
Poor sleep habits
Muscle tension

May be physically active
Often rigid appearance
More effected by Bio-rhythms
Tendency to overindulge

Emotion:

Chronic emergency tension—
Oscillates between inappropriate comfort to extreme discomfort with self
Irritable
Low frustration tolerance
High potential for depression and aggression—
Reactive—expressive
Addictive type—
Moody—driven—
Typical leader type
Sociopathic tendency
Sadistic/masochistic feeling tone——
Easy to disappoint
Can be hyperactive and manic
High autonomic reactivity
Bouts of self-pity alternating with delusional powers
Strong feelings of inferiority

Evaluate yourself as this type.
Where are you on this 7 point scale?
Excellent — — — — — — Poor

Return to the top of this list and check mark the descriptions under each of the categories which apply to you. Now count the number of check marks and enter the number here: _____

Type C Person:
THE HERMIT

Low Energy— High Tension—

Cognition:
Poor cognitive tone
Tension, poor charge build up, poor discharge, poor relaxation
Sloppy thinking
Believer
Obsessive thinking
Abstract
Poor ability to assess a situation and the resources available
Can be lost in endless abstractions and details
Very active fantasy life
Fuzzy blurred sense of reality
Poor body image

Will:
Passive, stubborn
A False will—reactive
Schizoid—Split will—fragmented
Average discipline
Teaches by repetition

Sensory—Tonic:
Often a waxy look—doll-like
Poor muscle tone, and a very deep core muscle tension
At times limp
Mixed responses to Bio-rhythms.
Sensitive—thin-skinned
Can be thin or very fat
Dysplastic physique—distorted body

Emotion:
Low frustration tolerance, easily depressed, non-expressive

Fuzzy sense of self—tense discomfort
Tends to hostility—passive-aggressive
Overtly Cold
Emergency tense—
Often addictive; prefers drugs over alcohol
Numbs feelings
High autonomic reactivity with instant parasympathetic reaction
Deep longing and self-pity
Inferiority feelings poorly compensated

Evaluate yourself as this type.
Where are you on this 7 point scale?
Excellent — — — — — — Poor

Return to the top of this list and check mark the descriptions under each of the categories which apply to you. Now count the number of check marks and enter the number here: _____

Type D Person:
THE UNIVERSE

The Average Man: Homonormalis

Low Energy—
Average Tension—

Cognition:
Dull Tone
Tension and charge, poor discharge, mixed relaxation
A conforming mind
Reactive thoughts
Can be very intelligent
Religious common belief systems
Can be analytical
Doesn't apply knowledge to personal life
Reflective of the 6 pm news

Will:
Common—stubborn, heartland—Mid-West life style

Sensory—Tonic:
Vast range of possibilities

Emotion:
Various
Can be comfortable with self or not
An often quiet sense of superiority
Can be dangerous
Can be addictive
In essence, average
Loud or quiet in conversation

Genesis 23

People like this are so common that they go almost unnoticed—they are more or less automatons. They are the conformists—slightly above average to below average intelligence—non-empirical, many beliefs, reflections of parental images......very susceptible to common Bio-rhythms......religious......rigid and limited, but with high autonomic reactions when threatened; poor appreciation. A quiet sense of superiority—you find them everywhere......

Evaluate yourself as this type.

Where are you on this 7 point scale?

Excellent — — — — — — Poor

Return to the top of this list and check mark the descriptions under each of the categories which apply to you. Now count the number of check marks and enter the number here: _____

Finally...

While I am aware that the number of descriptors in each basic type is different from each other, I would like you to return to the top again...... Ignoring the number of checkmarks, re-evaluate your overall impression of your self. If it has changed, use a different color pen and recheck the seven point scale for each type. Put this away for a week. Now take out another color pen and check each of the 7 point scales again. How stable was your evaluation? How did the number of individual checkmarks affect your second impression of yourself?

Now, here is the kicker: I want you to take from each of the four types those qualities that best describe you as you know and see yourself...... You may have to go back and give those descriptors additional check marks to reflect your perception of yourself.

Once you have done this: find a Tarot card which represents the type you have created.

This is your Genesis. From your Genesis pick those qualities which you would like to enhance or add, and those you would like to remove.

Become Who You Are
There Are No Guarantees

Become Who You Are
There Are No Guarantees

**To Know - To Will
To Dare - To Be Silent**

Part 2

THE JOYS OF REVENGE

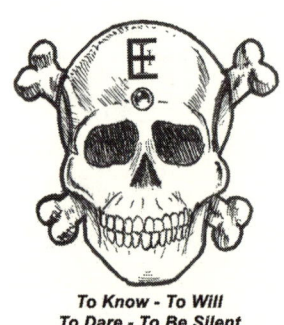

To Know - To Will
To Dare - To Be Silent

Make a list of all those people against whom you would like to take revenge, and include, in detail, the crimes they have committed against you. Be sure to include their type from the list above.

But first, take Revenge on Yourself.

You are the Enemy!

Make a list of the crimes you have committed against yourself.

Now beat the hell out of yourself—do a good job—this is the last time you will be allowed to be a louse to yourself.

On Taking Revenge on Yourself

What abilities do I have?

To get what I want?

To communicate my strengths and weakness to myself?

Do I have the capacity to "love" myself at my worst?

How aware am I of my intentions?

Do I pursue my intentions in some way everyday?

And the most important: How clearly can you see yourself?

Exercise: Each day, find a new way to show your will to become who you are.

Thought of the Day

The most important thing you can do on Psychopath's Sunday is to dig up another belief and burn it alive.

When you have no beliefs, you will have no more unpleasant thoughts. Of course, that means you won't have any pleasant ones either—

Thought-feeling matrices are a poor substitute for living— Enjoy……

Part 3

A DAY IN THE LIFE OF A PSYCHOPATH

*To Know - To Will
To Dare - To Be Silent*

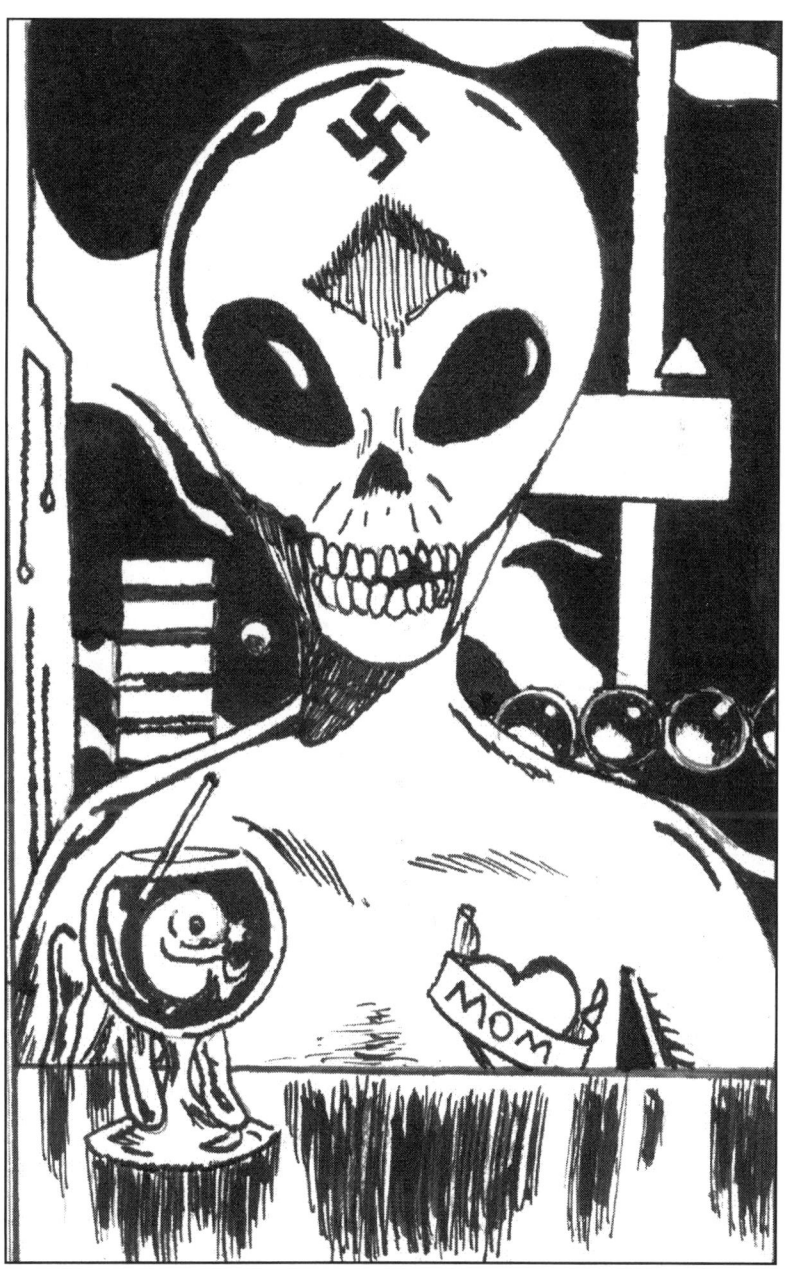

THE PSYCHOPATH'S DAILY PRAYER

I will never submit to stupidity or belief, and though I may lose a battle I will never be defeated even in death.

1. Each morning, begin the day with the affirmation:

"I will serve my highest aspirations with truth, strength and joy. I hereby bind myself in every way in everything I do throughout the day to my highest purposes. Everything I do, whether big or small, serves my end."

2. Each evening repeat the above affirmation, but include the phrase "even in my dreams I will affirm my goals, strength and power."

3. Refuse to entertain thoughts of self-doubt and failure—and ignore all those who attempt to influence you against yourself. Remember, each painful thought has an underlying belief.

4. Thank yourself each and every day and night for any effort you put forth to accomplish your ends.

5. Do not mourn over any failure or loss—do not dwell on losses. If and when you catch yourself regretting your errors......slap yourself in the face.

6. Build in your mind the images which reflect your future.

7. Start your day early and end your day late.

8. Do not overindulge in food, sex, or anything which will sidetrack you from your end.

9. Cleanse yourself every day from defeatist programs. Keep your body and mind in fine tune. Choose a different part of your body everyday and give it special attention.

10. Avoid talking about other people unless it suits your purpose. Do not become known as a gossip. Avoid participating in gossip sessions with co-workers or acquaintances. If you are stuck in a situation where this type of behavior is going on......only give tacit approval—avoid contributing directly.

11. Study something of value each and everyday, even if it is only for ten minutes.

12. Record a new idea in your journal each and every day.

13. Give at least one hour a day to private and quiet time—either in meditation or contemplation.

14. Find people who know more than you do—watch, listen and learn. Ask questions when necessary, but do not show off your knowledge or argue with them.

15. Each and every day record at least one sentence about what you have accomplished.

16. Make up a fresh affirmation and set of images when you are attempting a new venture.

17. Do half an hour of research in an area you know nothing about. Just read......don't force yourself to understand......turn the understanding over to your unconscious mind.

18. Perform even the most menial task with attention and concentration. Allow no opportunity to train your brain to pass you by.

19. GIve something of yours away each and every month. Attempt to find one person you can benefit—particularly if you don't like them.

20. Attempt to pass on the teachings of *The Psychopath's Bible* to worthy people—but avoid telling them what you are doing. If they ask for more assistance, tell them to buy the book.

21. Find someone or something that is beautiful and that you admire. Look at it or listen to it as often as you can.

22. Attempt to share your joy and success with at least one other person.

23. Watch your thoughts, actions, and speech for signs of self-betrayal.

24. Learn to love something, whether it is a person, an object, or an idea.

25. Avoid eating large meals which will dull your mind—particularly in the afternoon and before bed time.

26. Try to find a small group of people who are interested in their own self-development...... Watch, observe and participate—and leave as soon as you spot the group turning into a belief-system.

27. Although you have your final goals and desires, focus on what you are doing in the moment. Concentrate on each and every small task at hand.

28. Once a month, let go...... Indulge yourself, violate all of the other rules...... Simply have a good time, as you define it.

29. Do not rely on talent, beliefs, or any ritual—these are only adjuncts to continuous effort.

30. Take small steps toward your desires—don't demand of yourself instant success and recognition.

31. If you find you have enemies, learn to sidestep them—it is a lot cheaper than trying to destroy them or dwelling on them.

32. When you begin a new project, plant a tree and watch it grow...... You can do this in a park or other public place.

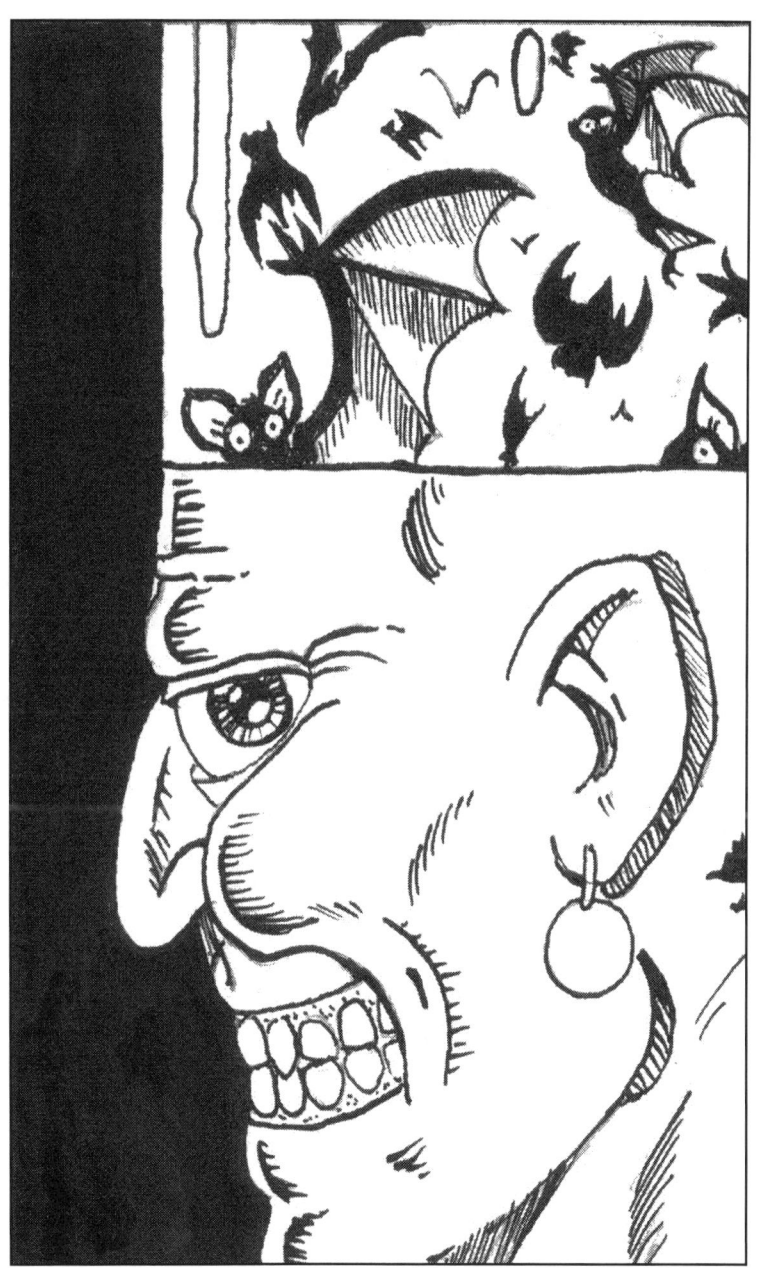

Part 4

THE SEVEN BLESSINGS

Often Called
The Seven Deadly Sins

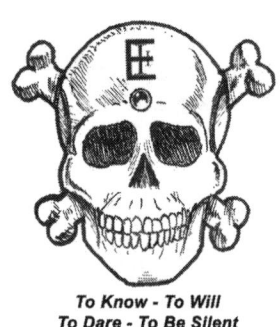

To Know - To Will
To Dare - To Be Silent

The Seven Deadly Sins
The Seven Happy Powers

God Favors the Bold,
the Strong of Heart

Be true to your own demon,
he who lives in silence,

Do not be swayed by the illusions of your emotions and attachments which come and go like night and day.

Beware all those who offer you knowledge without effort, for they implant within you what they want you to know.

That which you don't pay for is worthless......and often what you do pay for is worthless.

Trust no one who does not desire something which they value in return for what they offer—for they are fools...

Believe no one who is dependent on the favors of others.

Thus, trust not he that died for you.

For in the end you will find,
He died because he couldn't save his own behind.

Let Us Pray

This is what lies
on the other side
of silence

The seven deadly sins are heavenly blessings......
You have heard of anti-venom?
"the seven deadly sins" are God's true powers—
made in His Image we do exactly right.
The deadly sins if used correctly can make you great...

Learn them by heart and use them effectively, but unlike Jesus *you know* the consequences if you are caught.
Remember, God is at war with man—He hates you……
He hates himself but won't kill himself—just yet. Man's suffering gives him too much pleasure.
God is miserable
your pain is his antidote—
look guys he killed his own son. You get the point————————

joy drives Him crazy

To defeat god at his own game (he does like a good contest), he gave us logic, reason, intuition, instinct and science. These tools will make you smart: –hyper–intelligent, immortal and free to travel the entire universe……yes, if used correctly the seven deadly sins are seven blessings—and your success punishes your enemies—oh, revenge again?

Before we begin, remember that not all people are equally competent at these seven skills. The ideal would be to find seven people who are experts at one or more and start a "Deadly Coven." This is the true magical order, the rest are imitations. Just look at 'em—junkies, hairy, fat, frail—

LUST

Lust is blind, use it wisely.
God is Lustful—he wants everything. There are no limits to his lust. Look—he murdered his own Son and called it a sacrifice—frankly he didn't trust him. "Trust not thee who lusts after power."
Does God trust *you*? Sure he does……

Lust is possession—a weakness in self……in essence, lust is not real pleasure, but a failed attempt to rid oneself of pain. Lust is a created by deprivation, guilt and self contempt……no one is born guilty, but made so by those whose own anxieties have created a false sense of order with prohibitions and restrictions. Are you following in their footsteps—by polluting your brain?

Lustful behavior is often degrading and dehumanizing, hence *stress* lust in those you want to suffer.

More often than not, lustful actions lead to guilt and self-deprecation...... It is wise to encourage lust in those you wish to have an edge over.

Shame is the companion of lust. Individuals who lust after possessions, sex or love bring shame—and "shame is not of wisdom." Frequently they will trip themselves up in some important way as the wisdom of shame is to inflict pain.

Shame, guilt and pain is the ultimate game. Ever try to win with a masochist? Their only card is their own demise. Remember, the only power a child had in combating a sadistic parent was its own pain and death. And this is what mankind has done with its God.

GLUTTONY

Gluttony is an ideal form of killing yourself— deadening the mind and making you weak... This is the purpose—constipation of the brain...... Food is but one example, but most people are gluttons in most everything they undertake—nothing is ever enough for them... Urge your enemies on, provide them with new and better addictions...help them expend their resources on nonsense, showing off their pain to the crowd... As for yourself, avoid overdoing most everything except accumulating power to carry out your own plans and to live your own life.

People hunger for numbness—help them become numb. Sell it on the street corners, give it away at parties......help them buy bigger cars and houses.

Make them dependent on external devices—assure them that seeking status is a worthy goal. Show them how to save for their old age so their children will have a better life when they die—sell insurance to everyone. People are gluttons for suffering. They believe that the more they suffer, the better person they are—help them to be self-sacrificial—these types are both pitiful and ugly, but they do it with pride......

ANGER

God is Angry—he harms and punishes those who do not obey him.

But can *you* do that with impunity?

Help others to be angry, particularly with themselves and their life style.

Help people hold on to resentments and teach them ineffective ways of acting out their hate...... This will lead to both mental and physical disorders... Teach them to blame everyone but themselves for their empty and miserable lives... This makes them more impotent than they are. Teach them to throw tantrums, help them to feel shameful and guilty. This makes them easier to use and manipulate.

When used properly, anger is a powerful motivating force and so is hate... Anger implies frustration, the blocking of goals and desires... Anger helps you identify your real desires and can help you plan on how to achieve what you want... So watch anger, do not judge it—trace it to the frustration behind it and back even further...

SLOTH

God is Lazy—he creates things by thought-images, sounds and words.

Can *you* create a Universe by farting?

Laziness is nothing more than ineffective action. Regardless of how hard they work they are lazy. Their minds are clogged with truisms and beliefs. Teach them how to work harder by doing more of the same. Redouble their misguided efforts toward true laziness—teach them to wish wish wish.

Reinforce habits which don't work. Show them how their schedules and routines are signs of their true commitment to success and happiness. Offer them pre-packaged plans which will exhaust them. Have them buy everything that will make life easier for them, but for sure do not let them think—that will stop them from spending money on their *thinking saving devices*......

GREED

God is greedy, he wants what he wants when he wants it and gets it.

But do *you*?

Teach people to buy more than they want or need. Reinforce the idea that they need to protect everything they own. Occupy them with the idea that they can never have enough of things and that

Genesis

the more they have the happier they will be. Show them how much their neighbors have and how happy it makes them.

ENVY

God envies—he doesn't like competition and wants everything for himself and gets it.

Can *you*?

Teach people that envy is the motivation that will get people where they want to go. Let people know how envious others are of them—keep them buying lest they lose out in the race for happiness. People want to spend money even though they are fearful—it helps them feel powerful and immortal. They can own things, be in charge of things—all the time decaying and dying.

PRIDE

God is prideful—he loves compliments., worship and gets it.

Do *you*?

Give them compliments.

Make them more dependent on you.

"When Pride Cometh, then cometh shame."

Pride—sometimes known as self-esteem—is regarded psychologically as a positive and essential characteristic of mental health... On the other hand, thinking you are better than others is not, nor is conceit.

As a deadly sin, pride contains something more subtle: the simple pride in yourself as human. For within this thought there is a great danger: disregard for god-as-creator, the one who is responsible for all and owns mankind, his most noble creation...... Thus, pride in this sense is something akin to self-worship disregarding god as the sole and complete cause of everything. It ignores the premise that man owes everything to god. But man also *owns* his gods. What a shame.

Regardless of what most people might say, Freud and others recognized a primary narcissism in all human beings. In other words, a self-love or self-worship that precedes the so-called Garden of Eden myth. Man wanted to be like god and didn't want to be dependent... This is the essence of the fall......as god prevents man from eating from the tree of life, "lest they become like one of us," immortal...... The tree of knowledge gave man the power of knowing, but the tree of life would place man completely out of god's control... Only god is allowed complete pride as creator, not man.

Helping others to harm themselves with pride is simple: just help them take pleasure in their pride. Compliment them, assure them that they are acting too humbly for their own best interest. Help them to show off. Reinforce their innate belief that they are beyond destruction. Suggest that they take risks—chances which have a real element of danger.

Having fun and feeling strong...

the greatest Sin.

Made in the USA
Middletown, DE
15 June 2022